# PAINTING THE YELLOW HOUSE BLUE

# PAINTING THE YELLOW HOUSE BLUE

## P O E M S
## JAY RUZESKY

For Kate - (Braid)

A very good trade all around! Thanks
for having me in your class & for sending
to my folks. Thanks too for Georgie
Emily - a lovely book.

Here's to more good talkEese trades
in the future.

Good things,

*Anansi*

First published in 1994 by
House of Anansi Press Limited
1800 Steeles Avenue West
Concord, Ontario
L4K 2P3
(416) 445-3333


**Canadian Cataloguing in Publication Data**

Ruzesky, Jay, 1965-
Painting the yellow house blue

Poems.
ISBN 0-88784-554-1

I. Title.
PS8585.U94P35 1994     C811'.54     C94-930020-9
PR9199.3.R89P35  1994


Editing: Sharon Thesen
Cover concept: Angel Guerra
Cover design: Brant Cowie/ArtPlus Limited
Cover photograph: Martha Sharpe
Author photograph: Lucy Bashford
Printed and bound in Canada

House of Anansi Press gratefully acknowledges the support of
the Canada Council, Ontario Ministry of Culture, Tourism,
and Recreation, Ontario Arts Council, and
Ontario Publishing Centre in the development of
writing and publishing in Canada.

*For Lucy*

*And in memory of Adele Wiseman*

# Contents

## Deep in the Fields of Nebraska

## Parade

# Skating on the Dome of Night

I wanted you bare-breasted, snakes in your hands. I
wanted you somersaulting off the backs of bulls. I wanted
you swallowing raw hearts and rattling volcanic ash. I
wasn't going to be my mother or my grandma. All that self-
sacrifice, all that silent suffering. Hell no. Not here. Not me.

— Sandra Cisneros, "Little Miracles, Kept Promises"

# Sergei Krikalev on the Space Station Mir

> this is for those people
> that hover and hover
> and die in the ether peripheries
> — Michael Ondaatje, "White Dwarfs"

My name is Sergei and
my body is a balloon.
I want to come down. I
tie myself to things.

My eyes try to describe your
face, they have forgotten.
My ears echo your voice.

I am a star, you can
see me skating on
the dome of night. My blades
catch sun from
the other side of earth.

Days last an hour and a half.
No one else lives here.
My country has disappeared,
I do not know where home is.

I am a painter standing back.
I watch clouds heave like cream
spilled in tea, I see
the burning parrot feathers
of the Amazon forests,

3

ranges of mountains are
scales along the hide
of the planet, the oceans
are my only sky.

This is my refuge. There is
no one else near me.
Do you understand what that means?

Elena, I am
cold up here.
I hang over Moscow and
imagine you in our flat
feeding little Olga
in a messy chair.
When I drift out of signal range
I do things you
don't want to hear about.

These feet do not know
my weight. A slow
balloon bounces off the walls.
I do not feel like I am flying.

I want to come back and
swim in your hair.
I want to smell you.
I want to arrive in the world

and know my place.
Think of me. I am yours adrift.

Let me describe
my universe: I can see for years.

## Contact

A phone, ringing in the dark.

I say dark but I mean night,
I mean, I was seventeen and the phone
woke me from a dream in which I had just met
a beautiful older woman from TV
who wanted to do it in the elevator
because of my inexperience.
I say dark but I mean
the lights were out and the phone
was ringing. There was a clock with
LED readout glowing red like a cold star.
It was 1:09 a.m. A dog was barking
a few yards down, light from a street lamp
drew Chinese ideograms on the blind,
and a car pulling out of a driveway
made them jive across the ceiling.
There was a chair with clothes piled on it,
a siren faint in the distance.
The phone was ringing.
I picked it up.
She said, "Hello."
I said, "Who is this?" She said,
"Who is *this*?" She had a nice voice.
I said, "Why are you phoning at this time of night?"
She said, "Why are you phoning *me*?"
I was waking up.
"I didn't phone you," I said.
"I didn't phone you," she said.
I asked who she was again and she said,

"You first." We established ages.
We talked about the weather and the full moon,
about how on the roof of a large
building downtown a radar dish pointed
at a satellite in space and in
a small room six floors under the antenna
an operator was bridging the distance
between young girls and lonely boys
while we peeked out of our windows at the full air.
We said goodbye but I didn't get her name or number.
The next day my father ripped the cord from my wall.
It was night and quite dark.
The city hummed as if trying to remember a tune.

## Diatomaceous Earth

When you breathe in and get heat
and the landscape takes and takes
without asking you continue across
a part of the map geographical time
forgot to push glaciers through,
a player in a bad '50s western:
*The Badlands* starring no one memorable.
Red-winged blackbirds skitter toward
what must be a river somewhere.

If you could get there and plunge,
drinking deep through your cracked skin,
swollen eyes soaking up water —
it's water you need —
you might then return to the
place you parked, turn on the
air conditioner, drive the thirty miles
to Hanna for a cold beer, book in
to a cheap motel with a bottle of something,
satellite movies on TV.

But the earth gives back nothing,
crumbles in your hands
as you climb another awkward rise achieving vista.

Trillions of plankton shrivelled and died
here centuries before Whateversaurus did the same
and hid in the baked soil only to come out
smooth and sculptural, a giant
folk carving from another planet.

Somewhere in the depths of those hills
new beasts are stirring.
Your eyes grow weak in the sun. Water.

You will never admit it now. When you
set out earlier you were planning
on never coming back. This is
a stupid way to die. They'll find your
mummified body, slow-baked over a few weeks,
months, all the water pulled out.
Skin that crumbles when they try
to touch you.

# Totem

Behind thirty-foot glass, a spot lights
the expression no carver could have invented.
The plaque says you were an entrance
post, made angry to guard against
evils lurking in the depths
of your untouched cedar relatives.

Not that I know anything about
your spiritual significance.
Who's to say what work you've done?
How many lives you've changed by facing the world furiously.
But there's a price for living with a splinter in the heart.
Your echo in the museum window is pale.
No one says anything.

Why wouldn't you look sad, never having known
the pleasure at the end of extreme unhappiness?
You've been standing with arms crossed
for a century. In all that time,
you must have imagined
other ways of being, broken from your role and fallen
in love with a woman who passed
on her way to the stream every day.
And then outlived even her memory.

All those years weathering everything!
The wind's licked the paint off
your smooth-grained features.

Your corrugated face is a relic;
there's something of the martyr in
your sun-bleached eyes. Rain
is the only kiss that's struck your limbs.

## Life Giving

The charts show the progress
blood makes as it spills
through a body —
there's a sink up front,
remnant smells of burnt chemicals
and chalk dust,
yoga mats in the corner.

A dozen metal suitcases lie open
scattered across the floor like split fuselages.
The rest of the DC-10 can't be seen.
Bodies are severed at the waist.

The instructor draws a diagram.
Everyone cringes at the baby
part, wondering if they could
turn a child upside down like that or
cover its whole face and breathe
in infant-size puffs.
You stand with your shy partner,

touching him the way his lover must,
run your hands gently down
his chest to find the soft
spot on the sternum
where you bunch your fist
and pull and feel him
give in. Restaurant patrons applaud
your anxious embrace. A clump
is hurled from his throat.

ABC: airway, breathing, circulation.

Then his touch as he lays you
beside the half-corpse
and sticks
his finger down your throat
to move your tongue,
then presses on your neck to catch your pulse.

Having passed some sort
of test you sense new professionalism
as the two of you bend to
Resuscitation Annie.
You gently slap her on the cheek,
put a pillow under her neck,
tilt her head back and feel for heartbeat.
He pleads with the crowd to stay back,
assigns the 911 call to a
smart looking kid from uptown.
Together you start in —

his palms are stretched out as though
catching a fastball pumping
five times fast while you lean over
whispering breath into her waxy soul
but her china doll eyes stare up
and her lips, kissed like this by
years of hesitant companions,
breathe back without love.

## Scarecrow

"She will ride in on a breeze,"
he thought. "She will be tan
but delicate, strong-willed but
soft-hearted."

When she tumbled from the clouds
she focused on
a point in the distance
and he thought, "It's me she sees
in her future."

Dorothy said, "I'll love you all the way to Oz."

She said, "Follow the yellow-brick road."

She said, "Come on big boy
let me light your fire."

Munchkins gathered.

He was a hick, a nobody,
not a snappy dresser.
Scratchier, if you
hugged him, than your father's beard.
He wanted nothing from her.

He thought, "She's the Wicked Witch
not the girl next door."

She said, "I want to find your
needle, haystack."

And he said, "Nobody is going to spoil my dream."

## Polanski's Witches

dance around a cauldron.
Their voices are
choked symphony instruments
in a jet's baggage compartment.
Never to be kissed
or held they are the victims
of a mad doctor,
something gone wrong
in the chrysalis,
frogs spilled halfway
through the incantation.
Their breasts have been
stuck in vacuum tubes, their
skin flakes off like old plaster.

The director wants
no one to love them.

When they lift their rotten
skirts the cave stinks
of lime-sulphur seeping
down your throat while they
laugh and clap their crotches.

From their crack in the ground
they spread through the fog across
the green grass of Dunsinane,

they hunch like old trees suffering,
while the peasants parade
Macbeth's puppet head, open-eyed,
wondering where he went wrong.

# Ink Lake

Bats with silent sonar echoes
negotiate twilight waving like
gloved hands, frantic
to catch the attention
of one woman in a grandstand crowd.
She is studying some event:
tennis, cricket, perhaps just
two men. Like Greek
wrestlers, they lift white shirts
over their heads and drop them
on the end of the dock jutting
into the lake's evening.
They face each other, naked
and too similar. Each man
lowers himself gently through the glass
as if avoiding a jagged edge.
Then they are two heads
skating across a pond of ink.
The bats fly overhead and the sun
sinks further beyond the
horizon's reach. What
radar would tell them apart
if you were a bat, say,
or a woman, tired of watching,
coming toward them down the lawn?

## Sneaking into the Stephen Hawking Lecture, Then Sneaking Back Out Again

> Why don't we notice all these extra dimensions, if
> they are really there?
> — Stephen Hawking

Show me the room full of electric minds
shuffling papers. It's true, they all
wear tweed jackets.

I'm with a handful of idiots at the door
who think uncertainty is when we don't know
for sure.

Still, when all the scientists have filled
their styrofoam cups from the silver urn of
attentiveness,

the usher lets us sneak into the creaky chairs
at the back of the room.
God knows

why anyone would want to hear this so badly.
God knows. Someone with a beard wheels Hawking
to the front of the room.

Let the congregation rise, then sit,
let even the introductory remarks glide over my head.
The scientist's neck

attaches but does not hold up the head full of stars.
He seems to sleep through his own explanation of
*sigma minus infinity*.

A brilliant computer delivers his lecture
with the eloquence of a new American car demanding
the seat belt buckled.

Every now and then, his eyes open. He is
one of those paintings that look straight at
everything at once.

Teach me that time is a box we put things into.
*Things* are not what they seem. When numbers appear
overhead

my mind creeps out the back way, touching ground with
the world of fear and control I've been living in.
Enlighten me. I've fallen

in love with my best friend's wife.
I understand only that we walked by the river
Lassie once swam to rescue someone.

We heard trains: mourning some kind of loss, I thought,
but she said they were just wishing they were
somewhere else.

We sat in a wild place, tall grass by a glacier-fed stream,
thinking of fish we couldn't see, thinking of
the animals

moving in the forest's imagination across the water.
Maybe a river otter, anything more wild than
a cat with collar and bell.

Tell me all about antiparticles. I want to believe in
a parallel universe where three or four people can love
one another without flying apart.

A final phrase and the lecture's over, the voice
a bulletin saying if you didn't get it, too bad:
" That is all."

We sat together until the sun shifted off the edge of the planet.
I couldn't remember
the name of a single constellation

but we made up the stars we couldn't quite
make out. Ah yes.
So that is how you fill yourself with light.

# Mary Magdalene

After Scorsese's *The Last Temptation Of Christ*

He felt at home in a place
the weather seldom changed;
the colour of the sand reminded him
of somewhere he'd been once
on a holiday. At night,
before bed, they
made a ritual out of
sweeping the gritty remnants
of evening out the door.

Their bodies
were a temple of consolation.

He took Mary and the children
into the village
to show them off saying
to everyone who would listen
that he was Jesus of Nazareth
who had come very close to death
and so each new day was a miracle.
"Look at my wife, once the victim
of a thousand men.
Look at my children. Together
we have made ourselves whole."

They shopped past ripe fruit,
gourds of wine and olive oil;
the sun felt good on his back.
If one of the young boys got tired,

the older would hoist him
on high shoulders. Jesus tried
to memorize his good fortune —
taking in smells (burning sandalwood),
the difference between waves breaking
and those out deep.
Friends flocked to them for the
intimacy they inspired. Later,
Mary read to him until her voice
was a rhythmic dreamworld.
They wore the scars of passionate jewelry;
they used their bodies to
shape a kind of prayer.

Years passed. Jesus began to wander
in the hills near town,
his mind filled with people
hungry outside palaces trimmed
with gold, of hundreds of
restless souls alone in the smallest
rooms of their lives.

Without a word, he left:
was thrust back as if
transported by his change of mind.
Steel through his palms,
thorns tearing his forehead. He cried.
Mary relearned her previous unhappiness.
His children forgot him.
It was the first time someone had given up
bliss for grief and loneliness.
As he hung, becoming the memory who

would live on for thousands of years,
an aura that was the exotic richness
of his suffering surrounded him.
He was most alive crying out
in the moment before he died
and forgot all other relevant things.

# Come Out Wherever You Are

## The Waitress at the Day and Night

*All you need is one good witness,*
one face, silent as a movie extra,
who'll see from a booth at the back
and break, terrified, from his
usual role, come forward past

the cappuccino machine, reach over
the counter, grab the boyfriend
by the throat and say, "That's enough.
The lady's had it." At the start
of every voyage, Columbus picked out

a star to be like a guardian angel
but it granted no wishes only
stood vigil on the long clear nights
ready to shout out a warning if
necessary. You can get away with

almost anything if you're a good
liar but occasionally the gods
check on things and move us around
like snakes and ladders. All
you need is someone who'll

follow your progress and step in
if it gets bad, one person to love you
and another who'll watch over.

*June 10*

# Picnicker with Children Near the Trans-Canada Highway

*I have half a mind to smack you*

and the other half is out running

through a cluttered forest
holding hands with you far beyond
the gravel-lined parking lot
and the bear-proof lids

of rest-stop garbage cans — out
where the mind wanders and you can
play safely, away from
wild animals and deep water.

Half of me wants to abandon
you and never look back.
I could leave you to
face the world like *I* did.

The other half *is* you, kicking
and punching like a trapped bee.
There is a part of the brain
that ropes me to this picnic table
and another that drives us on
through mountain passes
without a second thought.

*August 11*

# Woman at a Schwarzenegger Film

*If I had girls it wouldn't be like this;*
this would be a love story and
these children cherubs,
blowing flutes, strumming harps
above jet streams and the sprawling city.
Girls would be thankful.

I guess it has to start somewhere, sometime.
Below the level ground of Iowa
a pile of spinning electrons bounces,
prisoners in a row of padded cells.

There are easier ways to travel back
through time. The rebel sends a guardian
to protect his younger self.
No one seems to feel any pain.

Maybe now a pressure builds
deep in the heart of my two small boys
who are anxious, who are on the edge
of their seats, who are punching and kicking
their way toward the end of the world.

*July 17*

# The New Neighbour

*Where the fuck do you go in this town to*
*get a good tattoo?*
You've got to paint the flags of vanquished
countries, the heroes of

forgotten movies — make your
one-time lovers indelible.
There are only a few things you really
need in this life:

one car to take apart and one
to put together, beer and vodka,
one day a week to sleep as late
as you want, and good speakers.

I don't care who you are you
can kiss my branded ass.
The grass grows up
along the fence.

Vines sneak around the
peach tree, wrapping my fresh
cut initials. I love the way
scars look when they grow over.

*September 24*

# Gambler at the Great Canadian Casino

*What's a little money anyway?*
Or a life for that matter
so easily given and more easily
taken back. And if the first

kidney was worth thirty thousand
how much could I get for the second?
Can a guy get by without urinating
long enough to win his way out
of a second mortgage, long enough

to break away from the loan shark
like a sleek, tropical fish?
Could I do with one lung,
one eye long enough to stake myself
back into a failing relationship?

And how would it feel to have
extra room in my chest cavity,
a space where something vital was,
just down from the beating heart
where blood flows, air sweeps in,
and luck, finally, runs out.

*July 16*

# What Was Left of James Dean

after he took the last
wrong turn doing over
one hundred miles an hour
breaking in his new Spider
on the way to Salinas,
after he bit down until
his tongue was gone,
wrapped the Porsche
around a Ford sedan like
shiny Christmas paper, was

a very relaxed thin film
of a man which these three guys peeled
from the cockpit like Wile E. Coyote.
They poured him
smooth as egg yolk
into a bucket and scraped
the asphalt with the kind
of spades you use
to bury people;
saw the last lick of hair
curled on his forehead waving
good-bye, that original
grin still on his lip,
neck twisted several ways,
his low Stetson back a spell
and they loaded
the remains of the car
onto a flatbed with a crane,
put the body in an ambulance and

all three guys (not used
to this kind of work) climbed into
the cab with a collective sigh,
buckled their seatbelts, and
drove him the rest of the way to Salinas.

## Black and White

The next day
the cop studied the ticket.
Looked at the J
and the line after like a mountain road
on a map.
He remembered workers in the onion fields
who stopped to watch,
their smiles as Dean signed the ticket
with extra flourish.
Remembered the silver Porsche
as it came off "The Grapevine" doing sixty-five
in a forty-five zone,
and slipped down the road like a spilled glass
of cheap whiskey, and how
Dean had pulled down his hat
and handed back the book and pen without seeing him,
had ignored his safety lecture
and accepted his thin copy of the violation
as if it were money, stuffed it
into his pocket and drove off into the sunset
as though the whole thing had been staged.

And the sergeant took off his gun
and set it beside him
as he sat down behind his unmoveable
oak desk and signed his own name
over and over on a piece of clean
white paper, Dean's ticket above and left,
so he could see the similarities
and differences between them.

## Bronchoscopy
— for Bill

The man slips cotton booties
over his shoes and stuffs
his scruffy mane into
a tight blue cap, like a
mechanic's only clean,
and wraps a white gown
around him until he is
an anonymous angel.

He snaps two rubber gloves
over each hand, follows
the surgeon to the O.R.
A woman looks up from her
stretcher and the surgeon
takes her hand and says, "No
problem," with his eyes.
She shakes as the nurses
roll her under the bright lights.
The anesthesiologist masks her face,
shoots something brown into her I.V. tube
and she dives into the still
water that flows
over the edges of the earth.
The nurses pull back the sheet
revealing breasts flat and round
as the lids of small pots.

The surgeon slips a hand
under her shoulders and lifts

so her neck bends like that
of a dummy you practise mouth
to mouth on; he pulls her
chin and the neck leans
more than it seems it should.
Someone hands him a steel tube
two feet long and he flicks
aside her tongue.
All of it goes in.
He peers through with
a light and finds what he wants.

The practical angel steps over
and looks deep inside.
African geese rise.
A herd of gazelles startle.
Three lions pad from the trees.

The anesthesiologist nods
and the surgeon slides long,
triggered forceps down the pipe
and brings out what looks
like a wounded bean.
He pulls out the pipe
and rearranges her head
on the pillow. Something
else goes into the I.V. and
she surfaces.
The nurses cover her,
speaking softly while her eyes,
as though following a bird,
spark and dart.

## Seeing Eye Dog

I have been dragging him
through the later part of his life,
careful as a new mother teaching
a child to walk, and I sit him
down on the front seat where
he can talk to the driver and
call out the stops judging by
the hesitation on the brake.

The passengers send themselves
into daydreams, rustling against
unfamiliar shoulders, twitching
like a dog chasing rabbits in sleep.
The bus sighs like a relieved horse
at the stops.
He backs through the door
like a retreating bank robber.

On the sidewalk his white cane
is a furious pendulum. Pedestrians
are ghosts. Invisible, they
press against walls
and hold their breath so as not
to give themselves away.
I lead him past.
Without a glance
we see everything.

## Petroglyph

They come in Volkswagens
off the main road and down
to where it's dark
except for dash lights,
with six packs of beer,
cheap wine. Always in pairs
and late, after a movie
or school dance, after pizza.
Carrying no flashlights
they spill down forest paths,
holding hands but single-
file: elephant couples through
the jungle. They light
bonfires even in summer.

In the morning you walk
the same paths
beyond the "Future Home
of Pine Ridge" through
the beautiful green stink of fir,
the cowbirds' gurgle.
To the place where sea-wolves
have been scraped slowly
into the rock, where couples
have spray-painted hearts

and initials over
frog-like birds,
their mouths looped open
in awe, in horror.

# Petroglyph 2

He works at the Confidential
Paper Destruction Company
shredding documents for the
government. He never reads
the things he pushes into the
machine, sliced bread coming out
the other side. He imagines
his own story there:
the words, a life.
The alphabet comes out
ready for ransom notes.

On nice days he walks to work
reading "Third-World Blood
Funds Your Lifestyle" in yellow
on a train bridge, someone else's
"CRAP" over that. And he sees
dog prints locked in sidewalks,
the fading script in graveyards:

knows the difference between hiding your secrets
and carving them in stone.

# Human Interest Story

> Determined to see baby, girls, 11, drive 10 hours with only atlas for guide.
>
> — Associated Press Headline

For two weeks they
pinched money from their folks
a buck at a time for gas and expenses.
Piled clothes on the seat to see
over the dash and
took off like innocent fugitives
tired of pleading their case.

The idea of them!
One leaning inches
from the windshield into
the wiper's desperate gestures
her shoulders hunched,
small hands strangling the curve of the wheel
as if a circus performer bending pipe.
The other straining against
failing light, looking for signposts.
The thought of them
as they arrive at their destination
the older sister at the door
expecting her parents
to unfold smiling from the car.

Her face when she realizes
they have emerged alone, alive somehow
from the death-chute highways.

A guardian angel? St. Christopher? "atlas"?
Some miscellaneous spirit.
These two girls, 11, peer over the edge
of a crib murmuring:
"Oh my god. Oh my god."

## Something About the Rain Falling on the Ocean That Sounds Like a Chorus of Missing Children

We were welcomed into this place
the way the ocean welcomes rain.
We are not alone. We have
left the schoolyard
turning to trickles of blue water we
seep into the indefinite corners
of the playground giggling when adults
walk by without seeing. Insects
bear us beautifully across the infinite
soccer pitch; dogs lap us up. We
are small enough to escape.
Take us out of your quiet living rooms,
away from Saturday morning
cartoons and cleaning our rooms.
We never asked for this much
love, our mothers' combs in our hair
weekday mornings. Take
our faces off the billboards
and every second passing car's
rear window. Take us off the posters
in bus stations. We are not lost.
Save us from your stifling
classrooms. Turn us
out of the boroughs of your imagination
where men with dark glasses have
tied us to the end of our lives.
Something about desperation
makes you know, finally,
you are alive: your loss is a pain

richer than the most
sensual pleasure. Stop looking
for us with small words.
We are liquid, flowing formless beyond
the prisons of our bodies. We would
rather come to you in your dreams.
Forgive us our absence as we forgive
you for needing us so much. Let the clouds
welcome us into the shifting fold
called heaven. Let us rain
down on the earth. Let the wind carry us.
Let us freeze and fall as snow to blanket the
sleeping houses of our families, let us
fall and melt on their praying faces.
Stop calling:

>       come out, come out
>       wherever you are.

This is a game, and we are winning.

# Deep in the Fields of Nebraska

the little burning boys
Cried out their lives an instant and were free.
— Theodore Roethke

# Roller Coaster

My father laughed and it was
the first and only time so far
I've heard him do it; a real
laugh deep from inside
climbing like an artillery shell
up his throat and pushing out of
his Edvard Munch mouth.
We were commuters aimed at heaven,
riding a steep, open train toward
the sun god at the end
of the line, padded straps
reefing our shoulders against
plastic seats. This was
the last place I wanted to be,
locked in like an astronaut,
someone else driving,
lunch rising in my chest.
My eyes were open to
the whine of pulleys as we
ascended a slope snow wouldn't
hold to if snow fell through the
ridiculous summer air. There was
a moment as we reached
the first peak and crested
when I smiled too at weightlessness,
the feeling as you float
from a swell in a fast highway until
most of me dropped. I felt
my stomach's desire
to stay behind up there where it could see

halfway to Saskatchewan and
to bail out again at
the bottom as we were
caught like eggs by a
giant hand and sent up again
over a short rise only to
plunge face-first at the ground
continuing as we rolled
through a giant loop, swooped
with the energy of descent and
twisted through a series
of corkscrew turns, our
brains in startled mobius,
my father wide with giddy terror.
Somewhere along the way he
reached over and squeezed my hand
and our astounded spirits
or some other part of us
that it seemed we could do without
for a while raced behind
like afterimages as we rolled on
through the inverted morning,
clutching each other,
wearing death-masks of happiness.

# Becoming an Atheist

What I learned then sustains me
through every sorrow:
it's the believer who keeps looking for proof.
— Anne Michaels, "A Lesson from the Earth"

Trains were magnificent
back then, sacred —
the legend of a country I
was getting to know.
When I stretched myself
along the ground
and put my ear to the tracks
I could hear
a rumbling as though
the earth was speaking.
Trees hummed like wires, water,
all kinds, had something to say.

I was eleven the summer my family
and best friend camped across Canada,
the airstream trailer a tin beer can
sliding over the map.
It was America's
two hundredth birthday, July 4th, 1976.
In my pocket, a special independence quarter
saved from the collection plate.
I had watched its flattened drummer
bounce off the tracks
under a coal and wheat train.
Where we stopped that night

there was a lame donkey,
its hooves swollen like
bell-bottomed pants.

Later, we counted a storm
in seconds: the flash, clap, and
roll until they were hysterically together
and the trailer became the rattling
set of a low budget movie.
A tree was on fire in the rain.

Next morning my friend and I walked along
the rail ties as if on stilts,
throwing rocks at the
power lines' blue glass connectors.
At the tunnel we dared each other to
go in through the rock to where
we couldn't see either exit.  If
the engineer saw us
he didn't blow the whistle
but white fear flowed
out the top of my head
when the light was there and
my friend wasn't and I pressed myself
against the cave like Spiderman,
the weight of the train
moving the granite wall,
diesel tearing my lungs like gunpowder.
I promised in that moment:
Dear God, if you
get me out of here alive,
I will not take money that is supposed

to go to you — forgetting
about my friend
until the train was gone.

I gave up on God.
And later that summer
I renounced gravity too,
pressed my ear to the track
where the last spike had gone in
and heard the Atlantic and
the Pacific whispering.
I had a whole life
to see my way through
and thought I might learn
to fly before I died,
maybe do a few other things
I admired superheroes for.
Spread-eagled on the ground
I decided I was not
horizontal but vertical.

My cheek was pressed
against the earth
in a loving embrace
and I hoped that
when my arms grew
and there were some
muscles in my chest
I could grip the whole
world like that
and move it a little.

## Ghost Stories

Something like Frankenstein
oozes from the green
spine. The worst power failure
Winnipeg has ever seen.
All afternoon winter has
dwarfed the city's passengers
behind drifts of fat-white snow;
businessmen hurl themselves
from entranceway to heated
entranceway just to make it
down the block. My parents
are stranded in Eaton's.
Snowplows are pushing their
way toward the centre
like yellow football players
under the dead web of bus wires.
The babysitter lights a blaze
in the fireplace and the room
becomes a place for
roasted hotdogs and marshmallows.
She lights candles against the dark
and we gather around like
forest creatures in Disney.
The bookcase is loaded
with political economics,
a dictionary with finger tabs
at each letter. She
opens *How to Succeed in Business*
and the goat-footed child eater
leaps from the book's graphs

I've seen in daylight.
I cannot see what else sneaks
out of the pages, threatens
spineless and laughing from
beyond the fire's glow.
My scream closes the book and she
holds me rocking slowly,
herself crying for
the fear she's put into me.

## The Nutcracker

We were six. That Christmas,
after the ballet our mothers
dragged us to, we sailed along
the 1A in a big blue Lincoln.
My mother drove and I
had to sit in the middle of
the back seat beside Danny while
he played with window buttons
and eventually the door handle,
and I thought about how
he buzzed in and out of
the igloo his father built,
how he wouldn't let me in
though I stood freezing —
when the icy gust sucked
him out, his fingers
caught the outside handle
and he hung horizontal at
seventy miles per hour,
loud mouth a cave, toes pointed
like a dancer's.
As we slowed, he did
the chicken-walk until
the car stopped. He was
in shock from gazing
through the entrance to some
darker, foreign world,
but his mother collected him
soft as a snowball,
and he went on living.

# Groundhog Day

They have no idea how fragrant and far down
Home is.
—— Don Coles, "Groundhog Testifies"

He is born again each year
from the bottom of a well
without wishes,
months in hibernation.

It takes a week to know
the dream is over.
When he wakes in the dark
he cannot tell
if his eyes are open or closed.

He rides his dark tunnel,
as though a nuclear secret
deep in the fields of Nebraska,

toward the white circle
that shines
like the entrance
to heaven.

He is not happy.

What can he say to reporters?
He knows more. He knows
too much.

Cameras boot up
and the crowd constricts
as if he were

Jack Nicklaus
and this
the eighteenth hole.

Their coffee grows cold
in the styrofoam
of February.

He predicts only unhappiness

turning from warmth and light
wishing, as any child would,
a return to the mud-comfort
of the womb.

And each year also
he dies,

reeling back from those
he cannot speak to,
digging again

his own grave through
soil, dirt, rock, dirt, clay,
past buried rusty tin,

until his shadow slips into
the folds of his gut and

the only sound is
his own heart beating like a fist.

## Ice Factory

While the fruit farmers of
the Okanagan Valley slept,
their sprinklers turning with
the hiss of snakes retreating to
the sagebrush hills; while
campers from Oregon dreamed
of emerging from water
to ski on it;
while high school friends rocked
the last remnants of their childhood asleep
with bonfires and bottles of wine before
moving out for good;

we sat in the yawn of bay doors,
desert night stuffing itself
around our machines.
There were long lines of punctuation
as we waited for water to
turn to stone. We smoked cigarettes
blowing plumes like iced breath
out to the heat-radiant parking lot.
We didn't say it was like heaven: an oasis
from the too-bright day. Instead,
when we talked, we spoke of
our friends or TV.

If I was there now
I would say something
about the girl he was in love with
who'd kissed my cold skin two weekends before.

Sincerity will always do even
if it's not impressive.

We didn't
talk about any of the things
we knew for sure.
In the future I would be the one,
sitting at a round table in the shade
with a pen still trying
to tell the truth in those
rare moments when I recognized it, still
thinking about the end
of our shift when we would
cross the warming beach together at dawn and dive
into the immeasurable depth despite rumours
that down near the bottom where it is
cold and always dark
there is a legendary lake monster
tourists on shore with high powered telescopes
are searching for.

## Single Mother's Garage Sale

This is a fear I cannot know.
I am looking at a woman
who studies me
from outside the elevator.

Earlier, maybe, in an
afternoon's back alley,
she is moving through
the shadows, past
green garbage bags leaking
grass clippings, past remnant
bits of car repairs, she is
walking toward the gauntlet's
end when a man appears
bypassing without acknowledgement like
a car on a Saskatchewan highway.

Then she is milling among others
on someone else's well groomed
lawn looking over tables of stuff.
She picks up what looks
like a cigarette case
but is a pair of binoculars.
The afternoon becomes surreal.
She turns them on
the house and it looks
like a nice house,
the sun blinks through
bits of the stucco's glass.
She can see the label on a

coffee pot; Melita, sounds
Spanish when she says it.
A stack of children's books
leans dangerously. Mostly,
there are piles of small
textile arms and bodies, empty sweaters.
She is admiring the garden,
strays off to study
camellia blossoms white as teacups.
Alone again she dreads the thought of
someone grabbing her from behind,
the acute distance between the
knife-edge and her throat,
raw places on her heels from
being dragged behind the
building, anticipates a bruise
on her lower back from cement,
red-black places around
her mouth and eyes where
he might stifle her with
snake-thick gloves.

She returns to the cluttered yard
sees a friend, sees several
friends around the coffee urn.
One of them drives her home
and stays on the street
until she is safely
inside the apartment. She
waits for the elevator,
its doors open to expose
a man looking at her.
She hesitates, steps in.

# Valentine's Day

Several stops after starting on the
way out for dinner I'm waiting for
the advance light on Main Street
remembering I've forgotten the wine.
The light turns green, yellow,
red again.
No one moves.
Same thing next
time and I honk
at the pickup
which is honking
at the station wagon in front.
I get out of the car
feet tightroping
the space between yellow lines.
The guy in the wagon is
twenty, maybe, his head
resting against the window like
someone trying to sleep
on a bus. A cigarette
burns its way between his fingers,
the ash empty as a bird's nest.
He is weeping, his mouth open.
People are trying to get into
the car, prying at the doors,
a cab driver is calling 911.
The part of me that wants to be
a saviour gets down on my knees and
looks at the place his ear is resting
hoping he might turn and

hear me saying,
"I think I know what you're
going through." An ambulance arrives
and we stand back. A cop is talking
to the pickup driver who *knows*
the kid is gone on crack.
They're taking my address.
His door opens like a vault
and I hear his radio tuned to
the "oldies" station pounding out
the kind of music we used
to listen to when life was
easy.

## Battle of the Monster Trucks

They bring in mud mud mud
from the country, load after
rich load delivered two yards deep
over the football field then
injured car hulls are pulled in
and lined across the dirt.

Three of us file through, stopping
for plastic cups of beer on the way
and take our seats in
the near-vacant stadium.
When the first trucks lurch out
I wonder why I'm here.

They are like angry adolescents
full of insult and noise,
bouncing into view arrogant
and torquey, exhaling like
pot smokers — they are as
we were some years ago,
wrestling for attention,
asserting ourselves whatever
the cost, testing our metal
against one another. Always,
in some subtle way, against.

When the light turns, the monster
trucks leap on stilted axles
listing side to side over
the row of crushed cars

ear-splitting noise and one
gets to the other side first.

And this is exactly where
I want to be, in the stands
with friends, aged slightly,
speechless for noise knowing
if we could speak we would
speak well of each other
while trucks climb themselves like
praying mantises, tractors pull
apart, and the incredible
dynamite lady blows herself up.

## Volunteer Gardening at Sunset Lodge

And now you notice your body
only when it hurts
and the mirror like an old acquaintance
has become indifferent and your
muscles complain after a day
of gardening at the Sunset Lodge.

When you were young you wanted
to get into the liquor store
rent a car achieve
a certain amount of respect
from people who by now are mostly
locked in low buildings
without stairs where everyone takes
meals in cafeterias.

You used to visit your grandfather
at a place like this where
the only toys were a set of
Russian dolls each small beautiful
body containing another small
beautiful body containing —

At the end of the day you
pour a long bourbon
feeling pain in the shoulders
and the base of the neck
that weak spot where
the old man in you waits
already hunched over.

## Painting the Yellow House Blue

It was always a place you could
go and be safe. The house
stretched its gables in welcome every summer.
You would take the plywood patches
from its eyes, start the pump
to bring water from the lake,
sweep the floors for cobwebs
and mouse shit. Whatever
puny beasts had moved in were shaken
out of rugs or chased back
to the foundation darkness where
you never played, imagining bugs
the size of U.S. marines repelling.
On the sills were the corpses
of flies and bees, the buzzing
long gone out of them,
you would vacuum,
holding the nozzle a few inches
above their dry bodies,
watching them fly again.

Now, they're painting the yellow house blue,
all the windows and doors
have been thrown open.
The house breathes.
Nearby, other cabins sigh in sympathy,
settle on their foundations
as the bruise grows. Along the edges,
the yellow siding is scraped and blushing,
a lone man hums slow, Muddy Waters

pouring out of his stereo.
He's painting the place
the same tone water has on maps,
shallow and even.

You would pretend to sleep in the bunkbed,
listening to the late lies of adults
drinking beer on the porch by kerosene light.
Sometimes there were campfires
and you could write words in the air
with smoke from the end of sticks,
whirling them, fatal, like trick biplanes.

The man is painting the place.
No one has lived there.
It is not a house where
someone played a badly tuned piano.
This is not the lake that was
dredged then, where they
brought the wet blue body of a child
and stretched him out on a
needlessly soft bed.
That was a yellow house
and this one is painted, different.
Not a place you would go.

Those were the years 1969 to 1973
when there was no news to speak of,
except the water temperature for swimming,
the choice between sailboat and canoe. Because
there was no other world then, just
the yellow house and a bit of forest

to disappear in, an endless
ebb and flow of visitors with sunhats,
food you didn't get to eat in winter,
your mother planting things that
never seemed to grow in all that shade,
other children seeking while you hid,
and your father, at that time of year,
saying yes to everything.

# Parade

# Hope

Hope is a small inlet,

a place where the river bends —
a quiet niche.

Is where the current relaxes
and everything goes smoothly;
fish gather to feed in sleepy reeds.

Derived from the Old Norse *hop*
meaning also hook, which may be baited
and lowered into the flow. Things happen
whether we want them to or not.

It's a tired little town
off the highway with gas stations
and motels near which
a mountain let go some years back
on the heads of night travellers and deer.

Fraser lost four companions
in the river at this junction,
they bobbed like lures
through the boiling rapids
and sunk breathless before the abundance of
what they'd been looking for.

# When Lucy Speaks to the Animals

I lie in the tub, ears
half full, soap seeping between
my lips as though to cleanse
impure thoughts as they form.

Her voice never quite arrives
as words but comes as a sort
of not very musical but
nevertheless comforting hum

like Ravi Shankar before
the "Bangladesh" performance,
the Western crowd ecstatic
while he merely
tuned his sitar and his
diplomatic response when he realized
they thought it was over:
"I hope you will enjoy
my playing equally well."

Her undertones rise through my
skin with the heat. My fingers are
raisins, body relaxed to the point
of complaint.

In California, scientists rip the leaves
from grapevines and check instruments
to see if the plants can really *feel*.
Small, sensitive mumbles emanate.

And above California alien bulletins
are picked up by NASA, gently intoned
from across the universe:
"We are coming, we come in peace."

## Primordial Soup

It is late summer and the beach
is nearly empty.
In a parallel universe
I am here with the child
I don't have in this lifetime
and we have come to where
the ocean brushes up against the continent
to study original life.

The sheet of thicker air
the water was before
I reached into it
sucks the skin on the hand
of my long lost body.
I wish for this child, want
to teach him to swim, for him to feel
sun dry the sea from skin.

"What's that boy doing to that girl?"

Near the bottom point
of the beach's moon-crescent,
two lovers are ankle-deep in water.
They have been practising
one kiss all afternoon.

The roaring volcanoes and the
shifting plates of the earth
are so loud that this child cannot hear
cellular life taking shape

in the warmest lake of my mind,
or that I am jealous of that couple
tangled in the rhythm of seaweed.

And now I am pointing at the sea creatures
in a tidal pool, naming them:
this is a limpet, it is a foot with
a hat which moves only with its toes.
This is an urchin, no you couldn't
swallow it. Those?
The green fingers of an anemone. Touch them.

And those two?
Three hours in the swim of love,
they haven't once come up for air.

## Crocuses

blooming under the trees, even
the beginnings of daffodils, tulips, the sun
arching a little higher: a bright kid
getting better at back handsprings, there were buds
on the branches I carved off with
a Japanese pruning saw, the shining
blade. And a glass cover over all of it that isolated me
from anything human, there was the phone
angry as a parent's voice calling
a late someone home for dinner, and him —
small malevolent god crouched
above the jar — how long it would take
the bug to suffocate?

"My greatest crime is the curiosity
that disturbed the progress of a snail."

There were the words of the Chinese poet. Me
dowsing the pile of prunings
with gasoline, the sparked
match and all the times I treated you
with less reverence than you
deserved, though what was lacking in those moments
was a lack in me too, there was my blaming
you anyway, and always the desire on my part
to hear in your voice the passion we left
behind somewhere. There were flames,
and spiders escaping, their world
heating up, and next door the two girls who ran
about the yard catching ash on their tongues.

## She Draws a Calendar

just like that,
an elaborate tictactoe
on the back of a menu
fills in the symbols of days
across the top and
stuffs numbers into the squares
each higher than the last
as if this were a game going badly,
the scorekeeper relentless.
"And this," she says, "is
the day I'll be back."

She draws out a combination
of moments that mean April,
describes the lines
that will be so many instants
of doubt and anxiety and fear.
She traces this container of days
in the time it takes her to snap
breakfast orders on a steel bin
and spin them at the cook
who looks back.
Their eyes lock.
There is such sadness
in his face, a whole conference
going on between them,
more in that glance than in
the Bible. He is saying,

"I love you dearly. Come
away with me and we will feed
on the flesh of exotic animals,
the fruit of trees with
Latin names and, afterwards,
banquet on the meat
of our bodies.
I will give you
all my recipes. I will
take you to where
the coffee is always strong.
Run away with me . . ." he says.

But the waitress is stone,
practical, pictures herself
on a Greyhound bus moving
like a pike in the
windows of buildings
steadily on toward
some former life,
a piano covered in dust,
a basement full of
playground clothes — because
she has decided *that* laundry
and those who put it there
would be a bruise to her.
In her mind she is already
being driven through the mountains

toward a man sitting at a desk,
the sun coming in to light
the contours of his face,

each full day of absence
X'ed on a grid above him and
above that this month's photograph:
a sacred temple's stairs

where ten thousand Aztecs a week
climbed toward the star
they thought was a god
and in the time it takes
to break an egg a wise man
peeled each humble believer and
sacrificed their hearts to fire.

# Three Dog Night

Australian aboriginals have a unique way of keeping warm on cold
nights. The more dogs they sleep with, the colder it is!
— *Adventure Magazine*

Twelve hours after
you flew off, our house
leaned from the foundation
into the wind.
The ocean lifted water
from a mile down the street.
The heaters quit. It snowed.
I didn't know which side
of the sheets to lie on,
shifting from one cold
arena to the other.
Wind chimes tied themselves
in knots and tried to crouch
beneath the eaves.
I searched out extra blankets
from the guest room
still shivering in the
unbelievable night light of the
sudden world outside
until finally I gathered
the dogs together,
one curled on my feet another
along my back, the third
spiralled in the curve
of my belly, taking pleasure
in the difference between

skin and fur, them liking
not so much me as the goosedown
tick, and we rode out the rest
of the night that way
all of us aware that
the body is never satisfied.

## Three Bears, Only Two

"The Modern Family" is
carved from sandstone
and mounted on a concrete block.
Round and smooth as pears, two
androgynous shapes
lean into each other.
Their arms like liana
bind them.

We drink coffee here
and the hum of the cafeteria
dissolves like sugar.

You give me this drawing
made when you were four,
preserved by your grandmother
over the decades.

On the yellowed page two bears
look straight out and seem
to be floating happily,
arms thrown upward together,
paws holding tight,
locked that way.

But no third bear roams
this lime-green grass
or rises up on haunches
to catch the scent

of watercolour-blue rays of sun.
The smaller one clutches
blossoms in one paw. Crooked love
rides their brown, oblong heads.

# Night of the Skagit County Parade

> in your most frail gesture are things which enclose me,
> or which i cannot touch because they are too near
> your slightest look easily will unclose me
> though i have closed myself as fingers.
>
> — e.e. cummings

I want to say something
thoughtful about the weather.  My body
is a medieval village and the wind
is blowing through it.
What right does the air have
to set this free?
But your fingers on my back tracing
the blades of my shoulder
nullify the draught's breath because lightly
*in your most frail gesture are things which enclose me.*

At four-thirty a.m. here
in the valley of eternal spring
you shift to the other side of the bed.
Your hand shuts and loosens.
Under the sheet's white page
we are paper dolls who tear
easily apart at fragile places:
our hands, cold-touching feet.
There are the blossoms of your body whose absence I fear
*or which I cannot touch because they are too near.*

Our own desire we recognize. To be desired
is something else. I thought you were

similar in this way: others' desire,
pardon the pun, is what we want.
In the afternoon you dug in the garden,
bent into the earth, your knees
leaving imprints of you there. I would not let myself soundlessly
kiss the sweat from your red shoulder.
But I stared, hoping you might turn and see
*your slightest look easily will unclose me.*

Now is the morning of the flower festival parade in
Skagit County, Washington. In an airplane hanger
luminescent floats look naked because cold has closed
the daffodils and irises that are their skin. Every
band member in red suede cowboy boots, all
baton twirlers, parade clowns, cheerleaders,  and singers
are opening tens of thousands of petals with their sighs.
Miles away we are blossoms curled inward from the cold,
and the idea of you opened by breath lingers
*though I have closed myself as fingers.*

# Acknowledgements

Thanks to Don Coles, Marlene Cookshaw, Sharon Thesen, and Patricia Young for wisdom and for close reading at various stages; and to Michael B. Davis and Donald G. Bastian at Anansi for seeing the book through.

Thanks also to the Banff Centre for the Arts for time and space, and to the British Columbia Cultural Services Branch for financial assistance.

Long live the following magazines in which several of these poems were first printed:

*Border Crossings*
*Caliban*
*Canadian Literature*
*Event*
*Grain*
*The Malahat Review*
*Poetry Canada Review*
*Poetry Northwest*
*Prism*
*Quarry*
*Queen's Quarterly*
*Secrets from the Orange Couch*

Some of these poems have appeared in a limited edition chapbook: *What Was Left of James Dean* (1992), published in Victoria, B.C., by Outlaw Editions/Press On.